D

Please return this item by the date above.

Education Authority

Education Library Service

Ransom Neutron Stars
The Rock Show
by Helen Harvey
Illustrated by Sean Azzopardi

Published by Ransom Publishing Ltd.
Unit 7, Brocklands Farm, West Meon, Hampshire GU32 1JN, UK
www.ransom.co.uk

ISBN   978 178591 432 4
First published in 2017
Reprinted 2018, 2022

The Rock Show

Helen Harvey

Illustrated by Sean Azzopardi

Ransom

It's the big night. I am wearing my leather jacket, black jeans and shades.

I look good. I look just the part.

But I feel a mix of fear and energy.

Tonight we play at the Rock Show.
It's the biggest gig in town.

"Jack! Come here!"

That's my friend, Kris. He is not much of a music fan, but he said he would come to the gig.

"I just got a text," Kris says sadly. "Jaz split up with me."

"Oh no," I say. In my head, I am thinking, *Not now*.

But Kris has taken a blow. He's not looking happy. I have to be there for my friend.

"What did she say?" I ask.

He shows me his phone.

Kris, it's over with us.

That's it.

"What happened?"

"I don't know," he says. "I was meant to see her yesterday … "

He starts his story, but in my head I am playing rhythms on my keyboard. Feeling the music.

I feel scared.

No, I feel fine.

No, I feel scared.

"Are you listening, Jack?"

"Er … "

No, I'm not listening. My mind is already somewhere on stage.

"She sent a photo of her new ring," Kris says. "It has a skull and a big stone. She found it at Camden Market. Then she called me and asked me how it looked."

"And you said?" I ask.

"I laughed."

"Oh Kris, no."

He looks upset.

"I know. It was a mistake."

I can see Kris is feeling really low. But my band will play soon, so I have to go.

"Sorry, Kris. I have to set up my keyboard."

Kris grabs my arm. "Will you call her for me? Ask her what I did?"

I sigh. This is not how I want this night to go.

With the band, I plug in my keyboard.

I pick out a riff. It's not long now until we go on.

I should help out my friend.

I get out my phone, scroll down until
I find Jaz, and tap the screen.

Beep beep. Beep beep.
Nothing.

So I send her a text.

Jaz, call me back.

And then it's time to go on.

A hundred people talk and jostle.

Forget about Kris, I think. I cannot help him now.

We start to play.

A hundred people stop to look.

They watch and listen. They move to the music.

Now I don't feel scared. I feel calm.
My fingers dance on the keys. I open
my mouth wide and sing.

The music makes me feel fantastic!

A hundred people yell and cheer.

It's over so soon.

It was a gig to treasure. I am buzzing.

After the show, I see Kris. Jaz is holding his hand.

"Hi, Jaz. What happened?" I ask.

"My little sister sent the text," Jaz says. "Sometimes she makes me so mad. Kris has nothing to worry about."

Jaz shows me the ring. It glistens under the lights.

"It's amazing," I say. "And the stone is so big. It's quite a rock!"

"Thanks," she says. "Your band were good, too."

Kris agrees. "Mate, that was special.

Tonight was the best **rock** show ever!"

Have you read?

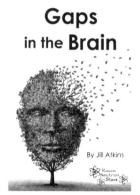

Gaps in the Brain

by Jill Atkins

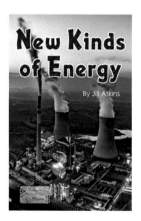

New Kinds of Energy

by Jill Atkins

Have you read?

G B H

by Jill Atkins

Platform 7

by Stephen Rickard

Ransom Neutron Stars

The Rock Show
Word count **527**

Covers:
Letters and Sounds Phase 5

Phonics

Phonics 1	Not Pop, Not Rock Go to the Laptop Man Gus and the Tin of Ham	*Phonics 2*	Deep in the Dark Woods Night Combat Ben's Jerk Chicken Van
Phonics 3	GBH Steel Pan Traffic Jam Platform 7	*Phonics 4*	**The Rock Show** Gaps in the Brain New Kinds of Energy

Book bands

Pink	Curry! Free Runners My Toys	*Red*	Shopping with Zombies Into the Scanner Planting My Garden
Yellow	Fit for Love The Lottery Ticket In the Stars	*Blue*	Awesome ATAs Wolves The Giant Jigsaw
Green	Fly, May FLY! How to Start Your Own Crazy Cult The Care Home	*Orange*	Text Me The Last Soldier Best Friends